Matt & Kelly

Thanks for the great meal &
good company

Hope Liam & Isla enjoy the book!

Peg Manuel

The Ugly
MOOSELING

Written by Linda L. Olson
Illustrated by Greta Gretzinger

Willow was born in early June. She opened her eyes and saw grass and flowers, then felt something rough and wet on her back. It was her mom, giving her a head-to-toe bath with her tongue! "Hello, Willow," said her mother. "Welcome to the world."

© Copyright 2012 by Linda L. Olson
Illustrator: Greta Gretzinger

ISBN 978-0-9755359-6-7

White Willow Publishing
4390 Kestrel Lane
Jackson, Wyoming 83002 USA
307-734-7002

Printed in China

CPSIA LABEL
Production Date 04/01/12 | Plant & Location: Printed by Everbest Printing (Guangzhou, China), Co. Ltd
Job/Batch #04809

Willow felt happy. Warm and clean, she drifted off to sleep. Willow quickly grew stronger and began to follow her mother. She stayed close by her side—the world was a big and surprising place!

During the day, Willow watched her mom eat leaves and twigs of willow bushes. She nibbled one of the leaves and wrinkled her nose. It was bitter. Her mother's milk was much better.

Her mom left the willows and waded into a pond. She dunked her head underwater.

"Mom! Mom!" Willow cried in alarm.

Her mother lifted her head. Dripping green stuff filled her mouth. She swallowed, then said, "It's okay, Willow. I'm eating water plants."

"Yuck," said Willow. "I won't ever do that."

"Yes you will," said her mother. "Wait and see."

As she grew bigger and braver, Willow began wandering away from her mother. There was so much to see! Jays cawed from the treetops. Squirrels scampered around the trees and rocks. Elk grazed near the forest on the far side of the meadows.

A coyote wandered by and saw Willow alone. He thought she would make a tasty meal. But Willow's mom was never far away from her curious child. She rushed up and warned the coyote, "If you come near my baby, I will stomp you!" He lost interest in Willow and trotted away.

"Wow," said Willow as she snuggled against her mother, "you're brave."

"So are you," said her mother.

"Wait and see."

Willow decided to make friends with the other forest animals. She looked up at the baby jays sitting on a branch. "Will you play with me?" she asked. The jays flapped their little wings and laughed.

"Play with you? You're big and ugly! We don't want to play with you!"

Willow was hurt and surprised. She left the trees and wandered over to a pile of rocks where the squirrels chased each other.

"Will you play with me?" she asked again.

The squirrels poked each other and laughed. A young one with a bushy tail said. "Look at you. You have a big nose, no tail, and long skinny legs. Why would we want to play with you?"

Willow sadly followed her mother into the meadows. A small group of elk calves romped nearby. *Well*, she thought, *they are more my size and look more like me.*

"Can I play, too?" she asked hopefully.

The elk calves stopped and stared. The largest one said, "Sure —catch us if you can!"

They gleefully raced across the meadow. Willow tried to follow, but tripped in thick plants.

"Clumsy moose can't keep up with us!" the elk calves scoffed.

Willow walked back to her mother. "Mom, no one will play with me! They think I'm ugly and clumsy!"

"Of course you are not ugly or clumsy. Every part of you is beautiful and important for a moose," said her mother. "Wait and see."

The summer days passed and Willow grew and grew. Her rusty brown baby fur turned dark brown. She ate more green plants and drank less milk.

One morning, she woke up and found the ground covered with frost. Fall had come to the meadows. Willow liked the colder weather. The pesky bugs of summer were gone. She grew more hair and stayed nice and warm.

As the days and nights grew colder, Willow noticed the jays leaving the woods. "Where are you going?" she asked.

"We have to leave," said a young jay. "We can't find food and are too small to keep warm. You are lucky to have a warm coat and lots of food to eat."

Willow knew the jay was right. Her heavy winter coat kept her warm. Her mother taught her to eat twigs and fir tree branches when the leaves had fallen off the bushes. She would not run out of food.

On a cloudy November day snowflakes began to fall. They fell faster and faster and the wind started to blow. The early winter storm lasted two days, covering the woods in deep snow.

When it ended, Willow watched the elk leave the woods. "Where are you going?" she asked.

"We have to move to lower ground. We get stuck in this deep snow," said the big elk calf. He watched Willow easily lift her long legs through the drifts. "I guess you are a lot faster than we are now," he said.

Willow knew the elk was right.

Two coyotes slunk by looking for something to eat. Willow was not afraid. She lowered her head and stomped her big front feet. The coyotes ran away! A watching squirrel called out, "You're brave, Willow!"

Willow looked up and recognized the bushy-tailed squirrel who had laughed at her earlier in the summer. "I wish I were like you," the squirrel called, "You stay warm in winter and can find food. You're not afraid of coyotes."

Willow knew the squirrel was right. She could live safely in the forests and meadows all year.

Willow looked over at her mother, who had been watching proudly. "You see, Willow?" said her mother. "If you wait and see, you learn that you are perfect just the way you are."